My Wild Woolly

written by
Deborah Eaton

illustrated by
Brian Karas

HARCOURT BRACE & COMPANY

Orlando Atlanta Austin Boston San Francisco Chicago Dallas New York
Toronto London

"Mom," I said.
"There's a Wild Woolly
in the yard."

I climbed a tree.
The Wild Woolly climbed the tree, too.

I ate a peanut butter sandwich. The Wild Woolly ate peanut butter sandwiches, too.